GW00360140

Postman Pat™
Annual 2002

Illustrated by Baz Rowell
Charlie Chalk illustrated by Ray Mutimer
Written by Brenda Apsley
Designed by Julie Clough

POSTMAN PAT™ © Woodland Animations Limited 2001.
Licensed by Copyrights Group
The Post Office's imagery reproduced under licence.
All rights reserved. Published in Great Britain in 2001 by Egmont World,
an imprint of Egmont Children's Books Ltd., a division of Egmont Holding Ltd.,
239 Kensington High Street, London, W8 6SA.
Printed in Italy.
ISBN 0 7498 5324 7

£5.99
UK only

contents

The Nursery

One spring day, Postman Pat was out on his rounds in his little red post office van. He saw his friend Peter Fogg putting up a notice at the end of the lane that leads up to his farm.

Pat stopped to say hello. "What's the notice all about, Peter?" asked Pat.

Peter smiled, but he didn't show Pat what was written on the notice.

"It's something new," said Peter. "You'll have to wait and see."

The next day, the notice was finished. It said NURSERY in big black letters, and an arrow pointed up the lane to the farm. "I wonder what this is all about?" Pat said. "There's already a children's nursery down at the school, and Peter's not a teacher."

Sam Waldron had seen the notice, too. "I don't think it's a nursery for children," he told Pat. "It must be a plant nursery. You know, Pat, the sort of place where people grow plants, shrubs and young trees, and sell them," he said.

"Yes," said Pat, "that must be it! Peter's nursery isn't for children, it's for trees. Sara wants a new hedge for the garden, so I think we'll go up there on my day off."

Pat and Sara followed the sign up the lane. Another sign told them to go across the farmyard, and round the back of the stables.

"I can't see any trees for sale," said Sara.

"The trees are young, so they won't be very tall," said Pat. "They must be behind one of the high stone walls."

Sara pointed. "Look, Pat," she said. "There's another arrow on the barn door, pointing inside."

"And there's Peter," said Pat. "Let's ask him."

"Hello," said Peter. "What brings you two up here?"

"Your new nursery," said Pat. "We've come to buy some of your youngsters."

"Yes," said Sara. "We need about ten."

Peter looked very puzzled. "TEN?" he said. "What are you going to do with them?"

Pat looked just as puzzled as Peter. "We're going to plant them in the garden, of course," he said.

"Yes," said Sara, "in a row between the shed and the greenhouse. Now, where are they?"

7

"In the barn," said Peter, opening the door. "This way."

Peter went into the barn with Pat and Sara. He pointed to a little pen filled with straw. "There you are," he said. "You can choose the ones you want."

Pat and Sara looked at each other, then they looked at Peter. There were no trees in the barn – just little wooden pens full of lambs!

Sara looked around and smiled. "We thought you were selling plants and trees in your new nursery, Peter," she said.

Peter laughed. "No," he said. "This is a special nursery for lambs.
Some of the new babies need looking after."

Peter winked at Sara and went to speak to Pat, who was still
looking a little bit puzzled.

Peter put a tiny lamb in each of Pat's arms, and handed him a
feeding bottle full of milk. "You can have these twins to start with, Pat,"
he said. "I'll let you choose the other eight yourself!"

Count with Peter

Look carefully at this picture of Peter's lamb nursery.

Can you find sets of 2 things that are just the same?

 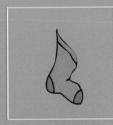 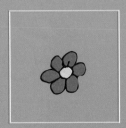  

NURSERY

The Greendale Village Quilt

1. Postman Pat and all the other people who live in Greendale have been working very hard.

2. They have spent all their spare time painting the walls of the village hall.

3. "It looks very clean and tidy now," says Sara. "But it's a bit ... well ... dull, isn't it?"

4. "I suppose it is," says Pat. "I know, why don't we put up some bright posters?"

6. Pat isn't sure about that idea. "It will be difficult to make sure everyone is on it."

5. Sara isn't sure about that. "What do you think about a big photograph of everyone?"

7. Granny Dryden has a much better idea. "Let's make a village quilt," she says.

8. "Everyone in Greendale can make their own special design on a square of fabric."

9. "Yes, I see," says Sara. "Then we can stitch them all together to make one big quilt."

WET PAINT

10. "Then we'll hang it up on the wall," says Pat. "What a good idea, Granny Dryden!"

11. Everyone likes the idea, and they all get busy. But they keep their designs secret.

12. Major Forbes uses some soft fur fabric for his design. "I need paper fasteners, too," he says.

14

13. Granny Dryden is knitting her design. She's using lots of different colours of wool.

14. Pat sees Peter Fogg when he drives past the farm. "What are you doing?" asks Pat.

15. "I'm collecting wool that's stuck on the fence to use on my quilt design," says Peter.

16. Pat sees Miss Hubbard with her paints. She's wearing her bee-keeping clothes!

15

17. "I'm going to paint my design on fabric," she tells Pat. "Then I'll fill it in with stitches."

18. Ted Glen works in his inventing shed. He does lots of hammering and banging.

19. Alf and Dorothy Thompson break up lots of eggshells into tiny pieces and colour them.

20. At the post office Mrs Goggins is busy with a kitchen roll tube and red paint.

16

21. "Now to get busy on our design," Pat says to Sara and Julian when he gets home.

22. Pat opens a big envelope. "Do you think we'll have enough used stamps?" says Julian.

23. When the squares are ready everyone meets in the village hall to sew them together.

24. They hang the big quilt on the wall. "There!" says Pat. "The Greendale Village Quilt!"

17

The Quilt Puzzle

Pat and his friends all made one square, then they sewed them together to make one big quilt.

Can you match Pat and his friends to the quilt squares they made?

Granny Dryden

Major Forbes

Peter Fogg

Mrs Hubbard

Ted Glen

Alf and Dorothy
Thompson

Pat, Sara, Julian and Jess

Mrs Goggins

The Best Blooming Statue

Every year, the villagers of Greendale take part in the Best Blooming Village contest. There are prizes for villages that have the best displays of flowers and plants.

Pat and his friends have worked hard. They grew lots of flower plants from tiny seeds, then planted them in beds, tubs and baskets all around the village.

Everyone had their own area. Mrs Goggins looked after the tubs and hanging baskets outside the post office, and Miss Hubbard helped the vicar to make sure the gardens near the church were filled with colourful flowers.

Pat was in charge of the village green. Ted Glen was helping him. They mowed the grass and filled the borders with flowers. It took a long time, but it was worth it to see the village looking so bright and cheerful.

Everything was ready on the day when the judges were coming to look at the village and decide who the prize-winners would be.

21

Pat spent the time before the judges arrived giving everything a
final check.

"The grass is neat and tidy," he said. "There are no fallen leaves
lying about. The beds and borders are full of flowers and …"

Pat stopped. "Oh, no!" he said. "I forgot to give the row of
stones around the edge of the green a fresh coat of whitewash. I'll
go and get it."

Ted looked at his watch. "It's much too late for that, Pat," he
said. "The judges will be here soon."

But Pat wouldn't listen. "I want everything to be just perfect," he said. "There's still time if we hurry. Ted, you bring the big bucket of whitewash powder from the shed, and I'll get some water to mix it with."

Ted went as fast as he could. But the bucket was heavy, and he was in such a hurry that he tripped on a stone. The bucket went up into the air – and the powder went all over Pat. He was covered in soft, chalky white powder. It clung to his clothes and his skin and his hair. He looked like a funny ghost with dark black eyes.

"Pat, we can't let the judges see you like that," said Ted. He looked at his watch again. "They'll be here in a few minutes. You'll have to hide."

Pat looked down at his white clothes and skin. "You're right, Ted," he said. "I'll go into the church hall."

But the church hall door was locked!

Pat ran across the green to the post office, but that door was locked too. Mrs Goggins had closed the post office early so that she could take the judges around the village.

Pat looked around for somewhere to hide, but he couldn't find anywhere. Even Sam Waldron's mobile shop was locked!

Pat was still trying to decide where to hide when he heard voices. The judges were coming down the lane!

Ted had an idea. "Quick, Pat," he said. "Stand over there on the green. Near the big flower bed."

"But the judges will see me!" said Pat.

"I know," said Ted. He put a string of shiny green leaves around Pat's head, and told him to keep very still – and very quiet. "Don't say a word, and don't move a muscle, Pat," he said. "Don't even breathe!"

Pat did as he was told, and stood as still as he could, holding his breath.

The judges stopped to look at the village green. "It looks lovely," said one of the judges, and she pointed to Pat. "I think that statue is the perfect finishing touch."

"Yes," said another judge. "We'll give it a special prize for the Best Blooming Statue!"

It's a good job they looked away from the statue then, because it was smiling!

Read with Postman Pat

Read this story with Postman Pat. The little pictures will help you.

Lots of leaves are falling from the  .

The  is covered in them.

 puts on a big , some

warm  and his  .

He gets a big  from the

and sweeps the leaves into a pile.

But a gust of wind blows the

up into the air. What a mess!

Pat makes another pile of  .

But jumps into it. What a mess!

 comes out with a of tea.

"Haven't you finished yet, Pat?"

she asks.

Pat collects the leaves in his  .

It's cold, and the is going down.

His  is red, and he sneezes.

Pat's sneeze blows the all over

the garden. "Oh, no!" says Pat.

Charlie's Camera

1. Charlie has a new camera. He has lots of bits and pieces to go with it. He's very proud of it.

2. He shows off to the others. "It's got a tripod," he says, "and lenses, and a carrying case."

3. Charlie takes lots of photos. Arnold has to squirt water out of his trunk. "Again!" says Charlie.

4. Mary the hover fairy has to fly over the beach all day until he gets just the right shot.

5. Edward is having a snooze under a coconut tree when Charlie pokes him awake.

6. "Wakey, wakey," says Charlie. "I want to take your picture. Smile please, Edward."

7. Charlie makes Captain Mildred pose for so long that she gets cramp in her arm.

8. Lewis T Duck has to do the same dance over and over again. "Once more," says Charlie

29

9. Everyone is glad when Charlie finishes taking photographs. They are fed up of smiling.

10. Charlie rushes off to Trader Jones's store to get his film made into photographs.

11. "Now we can stop posing and have a rest," said Edward, closing his eyes. "ZZZZZZZZ."

12. But Edward is soon awake again when Charlie comes back. He looks a bit embarrassed.

13. "What is it?" asks Lewis. "I don't have to do that dance AGAIN, do I?"

14. "No," says Charlie. "I was very pleased with all the photographs I took of all of you."

15. "Then what's the matter?" says Captain Mildred. "Where are they? Come on, spill the beans!"

16. "I haven't got them," says Charlie. "I forgot to put a film in my camera!"

Spot the Differences

Charlie took lots of photographs. These two look the same, but there are 5 things that are different in the one at the bottom of the page. Can you find them?

32

Pat's Plums

Pat has lots of fruit trees in his garden. There were lots of apples and pears on them this year, but the plum trees were the best of all. There was so much fruit that it weighed the branches down.

Pat picked the plums when they were ripe. It took a long time, and at the end of the day there were boxes and baskets of fruit all over the place. The garden shed was full, and so was the garage. Pat put boxes of plums in the cupboard under the stairs, and up in the loft.

Pat, Sara and Julian like plums, but there were so many plums that they got fed up eating them. They had cereal with baked plums for breakfast, and pork chops with plums for lunch. Sara made sausages with plum sauce for supper, and for pudding there was rice pudding with – plums.

"I like plums, but I am a bit tired of them," said Pat as he tried to pack another box into the pantry cupboard. "I'm going to give some of them away."

"That's a good idea," said Sara. "I can think of lots of people in the village who'll be able to use them."

Pat put boxes of plums into the back of his little red post office van. "I'll deliver them with the post tomorrow," he said.

Pat's friends were very pleased with the plums. He gave a box to Mrs Goggins at the post office, and took one each to Dorothy Thompson, Miss Hubbard and Granny Dryden when he delivered their post.

"What a nice surprise! Thank you, Pat," said Granny Dryden. "I'm going to have a nice morning in the kitchen making plum chutney."

Pat had a lot of mail to deliver, and it was quite late when he got home. There were three little boxes sitting on the kitchen table.

"Miss Hubbard brought them on her bicycle," Sara explained. "They are little gifts from Miss Hubbard, Granny Dryden and Dorothy Thompson to thank you for the plums you gave them. Miss Hubbard said they're a special treat for your lunch tomorrow. But you mustn't look in the boxes; they are a surprise."

Miss Hubbard is a very good cook, and her chocolate cakes are extra special. Pat hoped that there was one in the big box.

"Dorothy Thompson makes the best apple muffins in Greendale," said Pat, shaking the middle-sized box gently. "Perhaps she's sent me some."

Pat wondered what was in the little box. "Granny Dryden makes lovely cherry truffles," said Pat. "I bet that's what she's made for me. Yum!"

The next day, Pat did his round in extra quick time, then he sat down under a tree to eat his lunch. He could hardly wait to open the boxes.

Pat opened the big box and pulled out ... not a big chocolate cake, but a pie from Miss Hubbard – a PLUM pie!

36

There were some muffins from Dorothy Thompson, but they didn't have apple in them – they were PLUM muffins!

Granny Dryden had made some truffles for Pat, but they were PLUM truffles.

The only other thing in Pat's lunch box was a shiny, polished plum from Sara.

Pat couldn't face eating any more plums, so he was very hungry when he got back to the post office.

Mrs Goggins had a little gift for him, too – a plate of scones still warm from the oven. "Would you like some jam on them?" she asked.

"Not if it's PLUM jam!" said Pat.

Count with Postman Pat

Look carefully and count the number of things you can see.

How many  ?

How many ?

How many ?

Now draw them in the circles below.

red apples

green apples

yellow apples

The Plum Tree Game

Play this game with a friend to see who will be first to pick all the plums from each plum tree. Will it be Pat or Julian?

• You need a die, and 20 counters for each player. You can use buttons or coins as counters.

• Take turns to roll the die, and cover the number of plums you score with counters. If you roll a 2, cover 2 plums, and so on.

• The first player to cover all the plums in his or her tree is the winner, but you must score the exact number of plums left to win.

• You can play the game on your own, too.
Throw for Julian, then Pat. Can you guess who the winner will be?

The Bonfire Surprise

1. Julian and his friends Charlie Pringle and Tom and Katy Pottage are very busy.

2. They go all over the village collecting bits of wood and old furniture on a little truck.

3. They go to Garner Hall and collect a big old picture frame from Major Forbes.

4. Miss Hubbard gives them an old chair. "It's only got three legs, so I don't want it," she says.

5. Granny Dryden tells them to look in her shed. They come out with a broken table and a tray.

6. "There are lots of old bits of wood in my inventing shed," says Ted Glen. "Here you are!"

7. Sam Waldron gives them some wooden apple and banana boxes from his mobile shop.

8. They take the wood to the village green and Pat helps them build it into a big bonfire.

43

9. Alf Thompson brings a big sack of potatoes and says he'll bake them in the fire.

10. "You can use these apples for apple bobbing," says Dorothy Thompson.

11. Sara makes some toffee apples, and Granny Dryden bakes ginger cakes.

12. Julian and his friends work hard, and the bonfire gets bigger and bigger.

13. On Bonfire Night everything is ready when the Rev Timms arrives with a wooden box.

14. "Shall I put it on the bonfire?" asks Julian, but the vicar shakes his head and gives it to Pat.

15. "Will you light the fire now, Dad?" asks Julian. "It's getting dark, and we're hungry."

16. Pat smiles. "There's one more thing we have to do before I light the bonfire," he says.

45

17. Pat kneels down and pulls away some wood from the bottom of the bonfire.

18. Then he takes off his glove and puts his arm into the hole, as far as it will go.

19. Julian asks Pat what he's doing. Pat laughs. "Wait and see!" he says.

20. "Yes, I thought so," says Pat, and he pulls out his arm very slowly and carefully.

21. "It's a little hedgehog!" says Katy. "What's he doing in our bonfire?" asks Tom.

22. Pat explains. "Hedgehogs sleep right through the winter. A bonfire is a cosy place for them."

23. "But what are we going to do with him?" asks Julian. Pat points to the vicar's box.

24. "We'll put him in the hedgehog box, and he can sleep in a quiet corner of our garden."

47

Read with Postman Pat

It's winter time, and the is falling.

 plays out in the  .

Next morning Pat's  wakes him

up at o'clock.

He needs his winter  , but

where are they?

Pat looks in the .

"Where is my ?" says  .

"And where are my ?"

48

Pat looks in the . "Where is

my  ?"

Pat looks in the . He finds his

old and his  and his  .

"But where are my  ?" asks Pat.

Pat makes so much noise that he wakes

Julian. He comes down the and

points out of the . Pat laughs.

His things are out in the garden,

on Julian's  !

The Sheepdog Show

Every year, the villagers enjoy a day out at the Greendale Sheepdog Show.
Farmers like Peter Fogg and Alf Thompson put on a very good show.
They show everyone how they use their clever sheepdogs to move flocks
of sheep around.

They move the sheep from one field to another, and take them
through gates and over bridges. At the end of the display they herd the
sheep into little pens.

Peter and Alf tell their dogs what to do by calling and whistling to them. The signals tell their dogs where they want them to go and what they want them to do.

There are lots of other things to see at the show. Peter shows how he clips the soft woolly fleeces from his sheep, and Ted shows how he makes thatched roofs from straw. Major Forbes carves walking stick handles in the shape of dogs' heads, and Granny Dryden makes corn stalks into little dolls. Miss Hubbard gives a display of bee-keeping, and everyone enjoys the dog show. There's a special prize for the dog with the waggiest tail.

"Look, Sara, there's a new display this year," said Pat, looking at his list. "It says it's a surprise called Quackers. I wonder what it will be?"

Pat and Sara soon found out when Mrs Pottage came into the show ring with her sheepdog. But he wasn't herding sheep, like the other sheepdogs – he was in charge of some of Mrs Pottage's ducks!

"Well I never!" said Pat, turning to Peter Fogg. "What do you think of that?"

Peter was in on the secret. He had helped Mrs Pottage to train her dog. "She doesn't keep sheep, but her dog likes to be useful, so she's taught him to move the ducks around like a flock of sheep," he explained.

Jess had come along to watch the fun, and he watched the ducks with great interest – until Peter's dog spotted him. The dog sneaked up behind Jess and barked so loudly that Jess jumped into the air.

The dog thought it was good fun to try to herd a cat, and he chased Jess out of the field. Poor Jess had to run as fast as he could, in and out of the rows of stalls selling cakes and plants and clothing. The dog was right behind him.

When Jess spotted a tree, he knew just what to do, and he leapt up and climbed as high as he could. He knew that he was quite safe up there, and he looked down at Peter's dog as if he was saying, 'You can't catch me!'

Jess knew that although Peter's dog could do all sorts of clever things, even he couldn't climb trees!

Peter's dog decided to wait for Jess to come down from the tree. He sat at the bottom like a soldier on guard duty, looking up at Jess.

But Jess wasn't worried. He just curled up into a ball, closed his eyes, and fell fast asleep, purring quietly.

Run, Jess, Run!

Peter's dog is chasing Jess. **Can you show Jess the quickest way through the maze to the safety of the big tree?**

Merry Berries

1. Captain Mildred likes gardening. She's grown a field full of sweet red Merry Berry fruits.

2. Charlie and the others love eating the berries. But Captain Mildred has a warning.

3. "You must make me a promise not to eat all my Merry Berries," she tells them.

4. "Because A, I will not be pleased with you, and B, I want to make jam with them!"

5. No one dares to argue with Captain Mildred. "We won't eat them," says Charlie.

6. But Charlie and the others can't stop thinking about the sweet, juicy berries.

7. That night, they all dream about the Merry Berries, and wake up feeling very hungry.

8. One by one, Charlie and his friends get out of bed and walk towards the Merry Berry field.

9. Early next morning Captain Mildred goes to see her Merry Berries. But they are gone!

10. She rushes around the island. "Come with me, Charlie!" she says. "You too, Arnold."

11. She shakes Edward to wake him, and makes Lewis T Duck and Mary follow them.

12. Captain Mildred knocks on the door of Trader Jones's store. "Come outside!" she says.

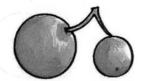

13. Captain Mildred makes Charlie and the others stand in a line. "Inspection time!" she says.

14. Captain Mildred smiles when she sees Edward's face. "Aha!" she says. "Berry juice!"

MerryBerry Jam

15. "Sorry, Captain Mildred," says Charlie. "We did pick the berries, and we did eat a few. But ..."

16. Charlie holds out the biggest pot of jam you've ever seen. "This is for you!"

Postman Pat™

COMPETITION TIME!

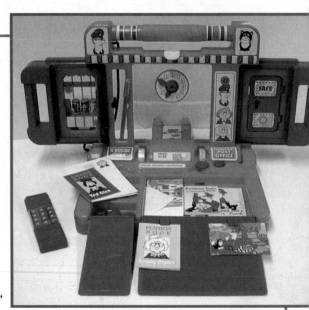

We've managed to enlist the help of Britain's Petite Ltd. and Racing Champions Corp. again this year, to supply us with carefully created, beautiful products to use as prizes.

We've got 4 super Postman Pat Post Office sets and 30 very special limited edition vans, in silver livery, to award as prizes.

The first four entries drawn will win:

Postman Pat Post Office

Includes telephone, ink pad and ink stamps, parcels, play food, play money, postcards, postage stamps, colouring book, pension book, note book, savings book, letterhead paper.

The next 30 lucky entries drawn will win a super commemorative, special edition, silver Postman Pat van. This is a one off limited edition van to mark Postman Pat's 20th Anniversary year and will become a true collector's item.

HOW TO ENTER:

All you have to do is answer this simple question:

Which anniversary did Postman Pat celebrate in 2001?

Write your answer on a postcard or on the back of a sealed envelope (don't forget to include your name, address and age) and post to:

POSTMAN PAT COMPETITION, Egmont World, Unit 7,
Millbank House, Riverside Park, Bollin Walk,
Wilmslow, Cheshire, SK9 1BJ.
to arrive by 26 January 2002.

Rules:

1. 34 winners will be chosen at random and notified by post.
2. Judges' decision will be final. No correspondence will be entered into.
3. The winners' names will be made available from Egmont World (on request) after 5 February 2002. Please enclose a stamped addressed envelope.
4. Employees (and their relatives) of Egmont World and their associated companies are not eligible to enter.
5. Entries are limited to one per person.
6. Competition is open to residents of the UK, Channel Islands and Ireland only.
7. The publishers reserve the right to vary prizes subject to availability.
8. Closing date for entries is 26 January 2002.